In Memory of

Caryn Rose Werthman

Text copyright © 2012 Harriet Ziefert, Inc.

Illustrations copyright © 2012 Smiljana Coh

All rights reserved/CIP data is available.

Published in the United States 2012 by

🍎 Blue Apple Books

515 Valley Street, Maplewood, NJ 07040

www.blueapplebooks.com

First Edition 03/12   Printed in China

ISBN: 978-1-60905-211-9

2 4 6 8 10 9 7 5 3 1

BIG BRAVE Daddy

Smiljana Coh

BLUE APPLE

Meet Charlie.
Charlie loves
his daddy.

Daddy
is big
and brave.

Charlie swims in the bathtub.

SO BRAVE!

His daddy
swims in
deep water.

Daddy is

Charlie's daddy skis down a high mountain.

Daddy is
SO FAST!

Charlie sleds down the hill.

Charlie's daddy climbs to the top of the mountain.

Daddy is
SO STRONG!

Charlie climbs to the top of the slide.

Charlie rides a tricycle.

Daddy is
SO SPEEDY!

His daddy races
his bicycle up
hills and down.

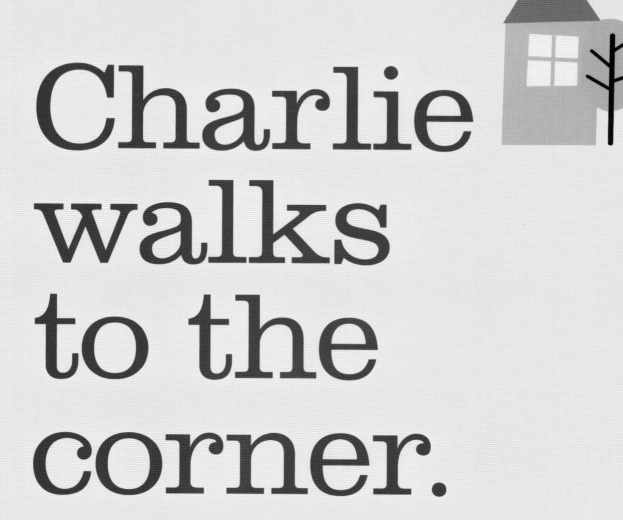

Charlie walks to the corner.

and SO BRAVE!

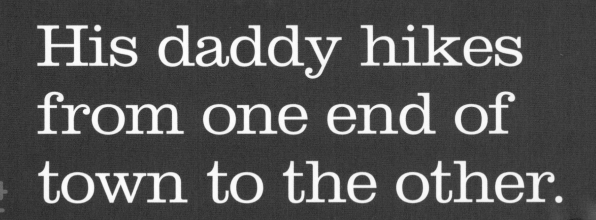

His daddy hikes
from one end of
town to the other.

Daddy is SO BIG

When Charlie grows up,
he will swim with
his daddy.

They will ski together.

They will ride together.

They will walk
the world together.